P9-DSV-901

THE GOLLY SISTERS
Ride Again

An I Can Read Book®

THE GOLLY SISTERS
Ride Again

Bladen County Public Library.
Elizabethtown, NC 28337.

Story by Betsy Byars
Pictures by Sue Truesdell

HarperTrophy
A Division of HarperCollinsPublishers

For Sis

—B.B.

HarperCollins®, 🐾®, and I Can Read Book® are trademarks of
HarperCollins Publishers Inc.

The Golly Sisters Ride Again
Text copyright © 1994 by Betsy Byars, Inc.
Illustrations copyright © 1994 by Susan G. Truesdell
Printed in the U.S.A. All rights reserved.

Library of Congress Cataloging-in-Publication Data
Byars, Betsy Cromer.
   The Golly sisters ride again / by Betsy Byars ; pictures by Sue
Truesdell.
       p.   cm. — (An I can read book)
   Summary: The Golly Sisters, May-May and Rose, share further
adventures as they take their traveling show through the West.
   ISBN 0-06-021563-1. — ISBN 0-06-021596-X (lib. bdg.)
   ISBN 0-06-444207-1 (pbk.)
   [1. Sisters—Fiction.   2. Entertainers—Fiction.   3. Frontier and
pioneer life—Fiction.   4. West (U.S.)—Fiction.]   I. Truesdell, Sue, ill.
II. Title.   III. Series.
PZ7.B9836Gop   1994   92-23394
[E]—dc20   CIP
                                                                    AC

❖
First Harper Trophy edition, 1996.

Table of Contents

The Golly Sisters Have Bad Luck

It was show time,

but Rose was not ready.

"Hurry!" said May-May.

"Get on your costume.

It's time to start the show."

"I cannot go on tonight,"
said Rose.

"Why?" asked May-May.

"Because we are going to have
bad luck," said Rose.

"How do you know?" asked May-May.

"There is a goat in the audience,
and a goat in the audience
means bad luck."

"I never heard that," said May-May.

"I have heard it all my life,"
said Rose. "A goat in the audience
means bad luck."

May-May went onstage.

She said, "People,

my sister has the idea

that a goat in the audience

means bad luck.

10

Would someone please

chase the goat away

so we can start the show?"

"I will," a man said.

He got up and ran for the goat.

The goat bumped into a lady.

The lady knocked over the bench.

Two boys said, "We'll help!"

They chased the goat,

and the goat turned around

and chased them.

Now everyone was chasing the goat
and bumping into everyone else.

"Stop, please stop,"
May-May cried.

But no one could hear her.

May-May came off the stage slowly.

"The goat is gone," she said.

Rose looked around the curtain.

"But May-May," she said,

"the people are gone too."

"Yes," said May-May,

"the people are gone too.

Sister, you were so right.

A goat in the audience

is bad luck."

The Golly Sisters at Talking Rock

May-May stopped the horse.

"Look at the sign," she said.

It said: ONE MILE TO TALKING ROCK.

"I would like to see

a talking rock," said May-May.

"I would like to hear one,"

said Rose.

May-May turned the horse

onto the side road.

"It will probably be the wind,"

May-May said,

"and we will just hear a moan."

"But it said TALKING rock,

not MOANING rock," said Rose.

"See. Here's another sign."

May-May got down from the wagon.

She put her ear against the rock.

"I do not hear a thing," she said.

Rose put her ear against the rock.

"Not even a moan," she said.

"I'll walk around the other side."

May-May heard a deep voice say,

"Rose is the best singer."

May-May said, "That is not funny!

I drove a mile to hear this rock talk,

not you, Rose!"

Bladen County Public Library
Elizabethtown, NC 28337

"It wasn't me," said Rose.

"It was the rock!"

"It was not the rock, Rose.

Now be quiet so I can listen."

25

E
C-1

May-May listened.

The deep voice said,

"Rose really is the best singer."

26

"Now that is not funny, Rose!"

said May-May.

"I am tired of this.

I'm leaving."

May-May got in the wagon.

Rose got in the wagon too.

"I know you do not believe me,

but it *was* the rock," said Rose.

"No, I do not believe you,"

May-May said,

and turned the wagon around.

Suddenly from behind them came

"But May-May is the best dancer."

May-May looked at Rose.

Rose looked at May-May.

Rose said, "See, the rock can talk."

"Yes, the rock can talk,

but it knows nothing about singing,"

said May-May.

"Or dancing," said Rose.

They looked back once

at Talking Rock

and drove away.

30

May-May Is a Princess

"I am going to write a play,"

said Rose.

"A play!" said May-May.

"Yes," said Rose,

"and we will be the stars."

"I like the idea, Rose," May-May said.

"What is the name of the play?"

"The name of the play,"

said Rose,

"is *The Princess and the Troll*."

May-May was quiet.

Finally she said,

"I do not like the idea."

"Why, May-May?"

"Because only one of us

can be the princess," said May-May.

"That is true," said Rose.

"And the other one will have to be

the troll," said May-May.

"That is true," said Rose.

"I can see myself as a princess,"

said May-May,

"but I cannot see myself as a troll."

34

"And I cannot see myself as a troll,"
said Rose,
"but I have worked out a way
to pick the princess."
"How?" asked May-May.

Rose said, "The first one to say
'I bid to be the princess—'"

"I bid to be the princess,"

said May-May.

"May-May, let me finish!

The first one to say

'I bid to be the princess'

AFTER I say 'Go,' gets to—"

"I bid to be the princess,"

said May-May.

"May-May, you have to wait

until I say 'Go.'"

"You just said 'Go'!" said May-May.

"I bid to be the princess!"

"May-May, play fair.

The first one to say

'I bid to be the princess'

after I say 'Go'

gets to be the princess," said Rose.

"GO!"

"I BID TO BE THE PRINCESS!"

they said together.

Rose sighed and said,

"I will change the name of the play

to *The Two Princesses*."

"I like that idea," said May-May.

"I bid to be one of the princesses!"

"I bid to be the other one!"

said Rose.

The Golly Sisters Have a Holiday

Rose said, "All we do is
sing and dance, sing and dance,
sing and—"
"I like to sing and dance,"
May-May said.

"I do too," said Rose,

"but I am tired of it.

I need a holiday."

"We have never had a holiday,"

May-May said.

"I need a holiday too."

42

"Then let's do it," said Rose.

"And not one word about dancing.

And not one word about singing!"

"Let's go!" May-May said.

She danced into the woods.

She sang,

A holiday,

A holiday,

There's nothing like

A Golliday.

"Wait for me," said Rose.

She danced after May-May.

They danced to the brook.

They sang,

A holiday,

A holiday,

There's nothing like

A Golliday.

46

They danced up the hill.

They danced across the fields.

They danced among the trees.

They danced back to the wagon.

"Oh, May-May," said Rose.

"We needed a holiday.

I feel good, don't you?"

"I feel wonderful," May-May said.

"Now I am ready

to sing and dance again. Are you?"

"Yes!" said Rose.

They got into the wagon.

May-May took the reins.

"Giddy-up," she said.

51

As the wagon moved along,

May-May and Rose sang,

A holiday,

A holiday,

There's nothing like

A Golliday.

The Golly Sisters in a Storm

"I hear thunder," said May-May.

"I hear it too," said Rose.

"I am not afraid of thunder."

"I am not afraid of it either."

The wagon rolled on.

"I see lightning," said May-May.

"I see it too," said Rose.

"I am not afraid of lightning."

"I am not afraid of it either."

"Remember when we were little girls?"

May-May asked.

"We were so afraid

of thunder and lightning,

we would hide under the bed."

"How silly we were!" said Rose.

"Rose, you know what would be fun?"

"What?" asked Rose.

"To hide under the bed

the way we used to," said May-May.

"That would be fun," said Rose.

"Let's hide under the bed."

May-May said,

"Remember how we used to sing

as loud as we could

so we wouldn't hear the thunder?"

"Yes," said Rose, "and remember
how we used to close our eyes
as tight as we could
so we wouldn't see the lightning?"
The Golly sisters closed their eyes
and sang.

"Who's afraid of the big bad storm?"
they sang. "Not the Gollys."
They sang again and again.

Finally they opened their eyes.

"I don't see lightning anymore,"
said Rose.

"And I don't hear thunder,"
said May-May.

May-May looked out of the wagon.

"Yes, the storm has passed," she said.

Rose smiled and said,

"I am so glad

we are not children anymore."

"Yes," said May-May,

"I am glad we are not children

who have to hide under the bed

every time a storm comes."

Rose took up the reins.

And the Golly sisters headed for
clear skies ahead.